WENDY QUILL
IS FULL UP OF WRONG

D1077863

WENDY QUILL
IS FULL UP OF WRONG

written by
WENDY MEDDOUR

with drawings by
MINA MAY (Age 12)

OXFORD
UNIVERSITY PRESS

OXFORD
UNIVERSITY PRESS

Great Clarendon Street, Oxford OX2 6DP
Oxford University Press is a department of the University of Oxford.
It furthers the University's objective of excellence in research, scholarship,
and education by publishing worldwide in

Oxford New York

Auckland Cape Town Dar es Salaam Hong Kong Karachi
Kuala Lumpur Madrid Melbourne Mexico City Nairobi
New Delhi Shanghai Taipei Toronto

With offices in

Argentina Austria Brazil Chile Czech Republic France Greece
Guatemala Hungary Italy Japan Poland Portugal Singapore
South Korea Switzerland Thailand Turkey Ukraine Vietnam

Oxford is a registered trade mark of Oxford University Press
in the UK and in certain other countries

Text © Wendy Meddour 2014
Illustrations © Mina May 2014

The moral rights of the author have been asserted

Database right Oxford University Press (maker)

First published 2014

All rights reserved. No part of this publication may be reproduced,
stored in a retrieval system, or transmitted, in any form or by any means,
without the prior permission in writing of Oxford University Press,
or as expressly permitted by law, or under terms agreed with the appropriate
reprographics rights organization. Enquiries concerning reproduction
outside the scope of the above should be sent to the Rights Department,
Oxford University Press, at the address above

You must not circulate this book in any other binding or cover
and you must impose this same condition on any acquirer

British Library Cataloguing in Publication Data

Data available

ISBN: 978-0-19-279467-3

1 3 5 7 9 10 8 6 4 2

Printed in Great Britain
Paper used in the production of this book is a natural,
recyclable product made from wood grown in sustainable forests
The manufacturing process conforms to the environmental
regulations of the country of origin

CONTENTS

Some legs: that are actually THE LAW

Nurse Hazel: sorting it all out

Me—Wendy Quill: in a special helmet

Florence Hubert: my best friend— in hers

Road Safety Officer

My amazing brand-new, second-hand bike

LESSON 1

WENDY QUILL

AND THE

SLIGHTLY-SQUASHED LADY

This is me BEFORE it happened

A very dreamy sugar mouse

Most of us have probably slightly squashed

someone. Even if we didn't know we

did. Especially if we were out on our

bikes and looking completely

the wrong way (you know,

sort of dreaming about

sugar mice and things).

But it doesn't always end in

3

DISASTER and the police don't actually always come. In fact, *sometimes*, slightly squashing someone by accident has a

REALLY HAPPY ENDING.

This is my favourite 'not-quite-so-new' red watch

Like the time I squashed a lady down the shops. I'd just been given a brand-new, second-hand red bike (to go with my not-quite-so-new red watch)—and was cycling to the shops for the FIRST TIME EVER, absolutely all on my own.

4

Swooshing professionally to the left

Swooshing professionally to the right

(The shops are much further than the brook and you have to go across two zooming roads.) That's why my tummy was all fluttery and I was feeling a little bit sick (but in a happy way). Dad had even given me some pocket money to buy some sweets because I'd spotted some rare birds.

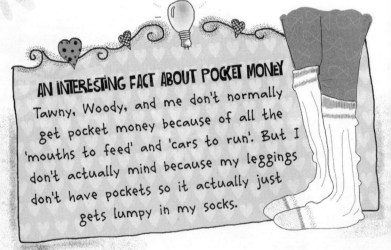

AN INTERESTING FACT ABOUT POCKET MONEY
Tawny, Woody, and me don't normally get pocket money because of all the 'mouths to feed' and 'cars to run'. But I don't actually mind because my leggings don't have pockets so it actually just gets lumpy in my socks.

Anyway, I was so busy dreaming about sugar mice and things (and trying really hard not to fall off), that I forgot to TINGLE my bell when I whizzed around the corner. And the corner was actually very sharp:

↓

↓

CRASH!

KERPLUNK!

WHIRRRR

'Ouch!'

I said, completely out
loud (because that's
what you say when
corners hurt).

Look! My handle
bars have even
gone twisty!

'Good heavens! What on earth
. . . well, blow me down!' said a voice
(because that's what you say when you
get squashed). I looked up from my twisty
handlebars. There was a walking-stick
rolling on the pavement and someone
else's legs all on the floor! I really didn't
know who it was, though, because all I
could see was a raincoat.

A completely mysterious slightly-squashed person

RR! CLUNK!

'I'm ever so sorry,' I said to the
raincoat. 'I hope that your legs are not hurt?'

'You really should be more careful, my
dear,' said the raincoat. 'In fact, I'm not sure
someone your age should be allowed down
the shops on your own.'

Something inside me gasped! Not
allowed down the shops! On my own! But
this was my very first time! Oh no! What
if Mum and Dad found out? Or even Miss
Pinch? Or maybe a policeman with a hat!!!
They might stop me taking Bathilda Brown
down the brook ALL BY MYSELF and
that would be like a nightmare!!! Without
actually thinking (or maybe because I was

NOOOOO . . .
you have to take
me for walkies!

10

10

full up of embarrassment and thinking too much?), I did a QUITE TERRIBLE THING: I picked up my bike, jumped back on, and whizzed away as fast as I could! I didn't even say that my name was Wendy Quill or help the squashed lady off the floor!

'Where shall I go?' I thought to myself, because I really needed a direction. I stopped and looked both ways. That's when I had the idea. I would turn left and pedal up the hill. Then, I would cycle to Grandad's allotment without stopping—no one would ever find me there!

A whizzing-away wheel

'Hello, Duck,' said Grandad, fiddling with the string on his beans. (Grandad calls me 'Duck' instead of 'Wendy Quill', but that is just because we are related.)

'Hello, Grandad,' I said back (even though his name is actually 'Pat').

'I like the look of your new bike,' he said.

'What new bike?' I said, pretending not to know.

'The one you just put in the hedge.' (Grandad notices absolutely EVERYTHING when he's got his glasses on.)

'Oh, that one,' I said, all found out.

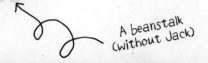

A beanstalk (without Jack)

W-H-I-R-R-R-R-R-R-R.

He came over to twiddle with the

chain. 'Fine piece of work, that is,' he said.

'Best look after it. Don't make 'em like that

these days. You can't beat a bit of second-hand.'

'Thank you, Grandad,' I said, politely.

'But it actually goes much too fast.'

This is how to check a WHIRRRRR

'I bet it does,' Grandad smiled,

spinning the wheel to check its

WHIRRRRRRRRRR.

I wanted to tell him all about it.

You know, about my slightly-squashing-

someone crime down the shops. I mean,

I *normally* tell Grandad EVERYTHING—

especially when I'm feeling full of wrong.

But then I remembered something important

A book full of criminal things

13

in Woody's *Big Book of Crime* and I didn't want

to get Grandad into trouble. You see, if you've

done something bad (like robbing a bank

or slightly squashing someone) and you tell

someone else all about it, then *they* have to

tell the police. And if they don't, they'll be an

'Accessory After the Fact'.

WHAT IS AN 'ACCESSORY AFTER THE FACT'?

I don't exactly remember and Woody's taken his
BIG BOOK OF CRIME back to the library, so I
can't completely check. But an 'accessory' is a
bit like a hairclip and a 'fact' is the same as
'the truth'. So I think it means that the person
you tell is like a hairclip after the truth—which
doesn't really make sense—but it STILL means
they might go to prison! And I didn't want
Grandad to go to prison because he's the
best Grandad in the whole wide world.

We don't want your tongues!

'Cat got your tongue?' asked Grandad,

because I was thinking and not saying words.

'No,' I said, not really understanding

the 'cat' bit (even though I want to be a vet).

'But I didn't knock *anybody* down *anywhere*.

And they *definitely* didn't get squashed.'

**'SORRY DUCK. CAN'T HEAR
YOU,'** Grandad shouted. **'I THINK
MY BATTERY'S CONKED OUT.'**

'Thank goodness,' I said very

happily, because suddenly my last

lie didn't count! I cuddled Grandad's tank

top quietly and listened to him shout.

'THING IS, DUCK,' he began (because

he tells me *EVERYTHING* too),

I still actually
want to be a vet
(even though I've
slightly-squashed
someone)

'I'M MEANT TO BE GOING TO BINGO WITH MRS BENNETT NEXT WEEK. BUT HER NEW HIP'S PLAYING UP AGAIN . . . SO I'LL HAVE TO GO ON MY OWN! DON'T FANCY THAT MUCH. NO FUN WITHOUT A LITTLE BLONDE AT MY SIDE.'

Not many Grandads can touch all of their toes

I smiled—even though my hair is mousey brown. 'I HOPE MRS BENNETT GETS BETTER SOON,' I shouted back (even though her hair is mostly grey).

'AYE, DUCK,' Grandad sighed, loudly. 'DON'T NEED TO WORRY ABOUT ME, THOUGH. LOOK! I CAN STILL BEND DOWN AND TOUCH MY TOES!'

AN AMAZING FACT ABOUT GRANDAD

It is an AMAZING FACT that Grandad can still touch his toes (even though he's older than the Queen)!!! Sometimes it is actually really lucky to have tiny ricketty legs, and toes that are not too far away.

'Wow!' I said. 'That's AMAZING, Grandad. But I'm afraid I've got to go home. I promised to clean out Benjamina's run because it's getting a bit full of poo. She's been quite nervous lately and hasn't been using her SPECIAL AREA.'

SPECIAL AREA

'RIGHT HO, DUCK,' Grandad shouted, not really hearing at all.

'I SUPPOSE YOU BEST BE GOING HOME?'

Sorry if Benjamina poos on your book! →

10.23

'GOOD IDEA, GRANDAD.'

So I very carefully pedalled home.

(I even remembered to use my bell quite

10.24

a lot so that no one got slightly squashed.)

And by the time I actually got to bed,

I'd forgotten all about the bad bits. In fact,

I probably wouldn't have remembered

10.25

them at all if a thing in the playground

hadn't made me **GASP!**

Ring your bell if you don't want to squish people

But pedal carefully if you already have!

The thing was a really tall policeman just standing by the doors the next day. **'OH NO!'** I almost-cried to Florence Hubert.

'THE POLICE! THEY'VE ACTUALLY FOUND OUT!'

FACT: not everybody fits on the page

'Found out what, Wendy Quill?' asked Florence Hubert (not really understanding at all).

'Found out about my slightly-squashing crime!' I said.

'What slightly-squashing crime?' asked Florence Hubert.

This is Florence Hubert finding out!

'The one that I did down at the shops! When I was dreaming about sugar mice and things.' And then I told Florence Hubert the WHOLE story. Every, single bit!

It's hard to
stop dreaming
about sugar
mice!

'Oh NO, Wendy Quill! That SOUNDS
AWFUL! Have they come
to take YOU away?'

**'YES, THEY DEFINITELY
HAVE, FLORENCE HUBERT!
WILL YOU PLEASE VERY
QUICKLY HELP ME HIDE?'**

'Of course I WILL!'

said Florence Hubert.

'That's WHAT best friends are for.'

She grabbed my arm like a

professional hider and we ran very fast

towards the bins.

21

The next page:
Me and Florence
Hubert hiding
by the bins

'What *are* you doing?' asked Sophia
Nowitsky, wondering why we'd just pushed past.

'Hiding from the Law,' said Florence
Hubert (because her Aunty lets her watch
late-night TV).

'Why?' asked Sophia Nowitsky (who
likes to know completely EVERYTHING).

'Because she's done a really awful crime!'

'Shhhhh, Florence Hubert,' I hushed. 'You're not
really even supposed to even tell!'

Sophia
Nowitsky
likes to
know
EVERYTHING

'Oh, sorry, Wendy Quill,' said Florence
Hubert.

'The policeman's not looking for *you*,'
said Sophia Nowitsky. 'He's come to talk
about Road Safety in the hall.'

24

'OH NO!'

I sort-of-nearly cried.

'I WASN'T SAFE ON THE ROAD. AND NOW HE'S GOING TO TALK ABOUT ME IN FRONT OF EVERYONE!'

'Are you alright, Wendy Quill?' asked Florence Hubert. 'You look like you're going to fall down!'

'Make a Friend' benches are VERY important

'I think I really am, Florence Hubert,'

I said, holding onto the 'Make a Friend' bench.

'Keep holding my arm, Wendy Quill,'

she said. 'I'll take you to the

part-time school nurse!'

'Nurse Hazel,' said Florence Hubert, extremely urgently. 'My friend Wendy Quill is not well.'

'Then you'd better come in,' said Nurse Hazel, who actually has a room all of her own (but only on Mondays and Tuesdays). 'What seems to be the problem?' She smiled.

This is Nurse Hazel on a Tuesday

'It's actually quite a long story,' I said, 'and I don't really think you've got time.' (I looked at my not-brand-new-any-more-but-I-still-love-it red watch.)

'Let me be the judge of that,' said Nurse Hazel. 'But first of all, where does it hurt?'

'All over,' I said. 'Actually, everywhere.'

'Oh dear,' said Nurse Hazel. 'That does sound bad. Could you tell me a little bit more?'

'I don't think I can, Nurse Hazel,' I said. 'Because then you'll have to tell the police. And if you *don't* tell them and keep it a secret, they'll have to take you to prison. Woody's book says it's THE LAW.'

A book all full up of LAW

Nurse Hazel sniffed into her arm.

'I very much doubt it, Wendy Quill. Not at *my* age. Now, can you please explain exactly how you feel?'

I looked at Florence Hubert.

'Go on, Wendy Quill,' she said.

'Well, the thing is, Nurse Hazel.' I chewed my lip.

BIG Book of Crime

28

"¡I ACTUALLY FEEL FULL UP OF WRONG!"

'Full up of wrong?' asked Nurse

Hazel, because it's quite a rare disease.

My lip wobbles when I'm full up of wrong

Nurse Hazel being quite a bit surprised

'Yes,' I very certainly said.

'Well in that case, you must tell me all about it. Why don't you start from the beginning?'

So I did. I started with the sugar mice (because I can't actually stop thinking about them) and my brand-new second-hand bike. Then I told Nurse Hazel about the whizzing corner and how I'd forgotten to tingle my bell. And then, I told her all about the awfulness: you know, about slightly squashing a lady and pedalling off without picking her up!

Florence Hubert gasped because I'd kept that bit all to myself.

Sugar mice get EVERY-WHERE. (Especially when you're trying not to dream about them)

'Gosh, Wendy Quill! That *is* a bad crime. And the squashed lady might even be dead!'

'Oh no!' I gasped, because I hadn't thought of that.

'That's highly unlikely, Wendy Quill.' Nurse Hazel patted me on the knee. 'Dead people don't normally say "Good heavens" or slightly tell you off, do they now?'

'No they don't, Nurse Hazel!' I sighed.

'Tell her about the policeman,' said Florence Hubert.

'What policeman?' asked Nurse Hazel.

'The one that's come to take Wendy Quill away,' said Florence Hubert.

'Yes!' I said. 'We saw him. He was waiting for me! In the playground!'

'Oh. You mean PC Lacey,' said Nurse Hazel. 'He's just come to give a talk in the hall. He's not going to take you anywhere, Wendy Quill.'

'What? Not even to prison?' I asked.

'*Definitely* not to prison,' said Nurse Hazel, grinning and standing up. 'Now then, girls. I think you two should go and listen to what PC Lacey has to say. It might actually do you both some good.'

'Does that mean I'm totally better?'

I don't really want to go to prison

32

I asked. 'That I'm not **FULL UP OF WRONG** any more?'

'Yes, dear,' Nurse Hazel nodded. 'You're just a little bit bruised.'

'Oh, thank you, Nurse Hazel,' I smiled happily, completely and totally cured.

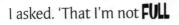

Even though PC Lacey was quite tall (and even taller with his helmet on), he was actually very funny and knew lots of REALLY IMPORTANT FACTS.

Here are some I quickly wrote down:

A very tall policeman with a head that doesn't fit

PC LACEY'S ROAD SAFETY FACTS
(WITH SOME EXTRA BITS STUCK IN BY WENDY QUILL)

1) Always find a safe place to cross.

2) Look left and right before stepping off the curb.

3) Don't think about sugar mice at all.

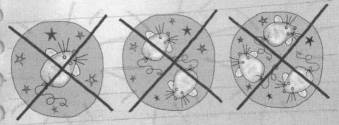

4) Never run on roads.

5) Listen with both of your ears.

6) Be very careful when you whizz round corners.

7) Always ring your bell.

8) If you squash someone, please remember to pick them up.

He even gave us special 'reflector triangles' to hang on the back of our bags (you know, the ones that go all twinkly in the dark). Florence Hubert was VERY impressed and didn't try to whisper even once!

'Wendy Quill,' she said, all wonderingly. 'I don't think I actually want to be a hairdresser any more.' We shuffled out of the hall.

'But you've always wanted to be a hairdresser,' I said, all full of surprise.

'I know,' said Florence Hubert, twiddling with her curls. 'But now I've met PC Lacey, I think I want to be a Road Safety Officer and help to save children's lives.'

I love triangles that are completely free!

35

'Wow!' I sighed. 'That *does* sound like a VERY important job.'

'Yes, it does,' nodded Florence Hubert. 'And I might even get my own SPECIAL HELMET. It will make me look ever so tall.'

Road Safety Officer

When I (accidentally) dream about sugar mice, Florence Hubert dreams about being tall

36

Then, all full of exciting Road
Safety thoughts, we single-filed
neatly back to class.

Miss Pinch was marking
things on her desk. 'Are you feeling
better now, Wendy Quill?' she asked. 'Sophia
Nowitsky said you'd gone to see the Nurse?'

'That is true, Miss Pinch,' I replied.

'What was the matter?' she asked.
'Tummy playing up? Or was it something
else?'

Miss
Pinch likes
to know
what's
going on

'Something else, Miss Pinch.'

'What? A headache?' asked Miss Pinch.

'No. I was just feeling full up of wrong.
But Nurse Hazel has made me all right.'

37

WENDY QUILL IS FULL UP OF WRONG

That night, Grandad came round for

dinner. But he didn't really say very much.

In fact, he mostly stared at the wall.

'Is Grandad all right?' asked Tawny.

'He's acting a little bit weird.'

'I was thinking the very same, Tawny,'

whispered Mum. 'He doesn't seem quite

himself.'

'Grandad's definitely himself,' I said,

wondering who else he could be. 'It's just

that his battery's all conked out.'

'Yes. We can see that, *Wheezy*

Bird,' said Dad (who'd just come home

from work).

NOT
HIMSELF

I don't like
Grandad's battery
being conked out

AN IMPORTANT 'WHEEZY BIRD' NOTE

Just incase you don't know, even though you probably do, 'Wheezy Bird' is my nickname because of the way I laugh. A sort of 'giggle-wheeze, giggle-wheeze'. I can't actually help it. It's just the noise that comes out when things are funny.

'But *why's* he all grumpy?' asked Woody, looking up from his book about Magic Tricks.

'Oh,' I said, because I knew already. 'It's because he's got Bingo tonight but Mrs Bennett and her new hip can't go.'

'Poor old Grandad,' said Woody, flicking some cards on the floor.

Learn to amaze!

MAGIC TRICKS

A very mysterious book!

39

'What shall we do?' asked Tawny. We all tried to think really hard. But we *didn't* have to do anything because suddenly the doorbell DINGED.

It was Mrs Bennett with lipstick on and everything.

'Ooh, hello everyone', cooed Mrs Bennett. 'I've just come looking for Pat.'

'GRANDAD,' I shouted, running over and patting his tank top. 'It's Mrs Bennett—she's just come looking for you!'

'YOU WHAT, DUCK?'

Grandad blinked.

Mrs Bennett smelt all soapy and purple

'IT'S MRS BENNETT,'

we all shouted back.

'SHE'S JUST COME LOOKING FOR YOU!'

'H . . . h . . . hang on a minute,' stuttered Grandad. 'I'll pop this new battery in. Mrs Bennett, you say?' He fiddled with his ear.

41

'YES!'
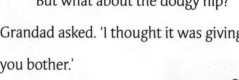

We all shouted again.

Mrs Bennett bustled into the lounge.

'Hello, Pat,' smiled Mrs Bennett. 'Bet you didn't think you'd see me tonight!'

'Evening, Mrs Bennett,' Grandad grinned. 'No. I thought you'd had to stand me up.'

'Oh no, Pat. Not if I can help it,' said Mrs Bennett, smelling of perfume and soap.

'But what about the dodgy hip?' Grandad asked. 'I thought it was giving you bother.'

Mrs Bennett and her handbag sat down.
'Well, you'll never guess what happened
down the shops, Pat,' she said. 'I was hobbling
along with that ghastly stick. Off to buy
a paper, like you do. When *some* young
whippersnapper came flying round that corner on their bike and knocked me flat!'

'Knocked you flat!' said Grandad,
in surprise.

43

'Yes, Pat,' said Mrs Bennett. 'Flat out on the floor. Like a pancake, I was!'

'Oh dear!' said Mum, because she cares.

Suddenly, Mrs Bennett looked at me. 'I think she'd have been about your size, Wendy Quill. But *you* haven't got a bike. And I know you're not allowed down the shops. Not on your own. Anyway, the funniest thing happened. When I got up, my new hip slotted right back into place—would you believe it?! Since then, I've never felt so good! Come on, Pat! Let's hop on that bus! I've got my free pass. We can go to the Bingo after all.'

Tossing pancakes is one of my favourite hobbies

. . . even when they land on the floor (like Mrs Bennett)

Grandad winked at me and scruffled my hair: 'Haven't got a bike, hey Duck?' he said. 'Here you go. Have yourself a mintoe. Now then, Mrs Bennett, give me your arm. Just in case another bike comes our way.'

The mintoe before it was sucked

'Ooh Pat, you're such a gentleman,' Mrs Bennett laughed. Then they walked completely normally through the door!

'What was that all about?' asked Mum.

Mum is busy wondering again

My cheeks went quite fizzy and red. 'Well, I didn't actually want to tell you,' I said, sucking my mintoe hard. 'You know, in case you *didn't* tell the police. And then you'd have had to go to prison and everything. But Nurse Hazel said that wouldn't really happen. And Mrs Bennett is fixed and is really fine.'

'What *are* you talking about, *Wheezy Bird?*' asked Dad. So I told them all about it. About the sharp corner and the sugar mice. About squashing Mrs Bennett on my brand-new second-hand red bike. And about not picking her up and feeling all full up of wrong!

Dad laughed. 'Well, I don't think you were full up of wrong, *Wheezy Bird.* In fact, you could say you were **FULL UP OF RIGHT**! Without you and your slightly-squashing crime, there'd have been no Bingo tonight. Not with Mrs Bennett, anyway.'

Tawny and Woody both laughed. 'Good old *Wheezy Bird*,' they said.

Remember to tell your Dad EVERYTHING

46

Woody, my big brother, doesn't laugh like a sea-lion

'Does that mean I can still go down the shops?' I asked. 'Completely all on my own?'

'Yes,' smiled Mum. 'As long as you always say sorry when you bump into people and remember to pick them up!' I nodded because I always will.

Nor does my big sister, Tawny

'And one more thing,' said Mum, stroking my mousey brown hair. I listened very carefully because mums are always right:

'Ring your bell on sharp corners . . . and try not to dream about sugar mice!'

THE MORAL OF THIS TALE

Don't worry if you slightly-squash someone down at the shops. You might still have a HAPPY ENDING!

Completely the RIGHT flapjack

Jemima Button: the WRONG Jemima

Me—Wendy Quill: telling a slightly dreadful lie!

Completely the WRONG house

Jemima Topps: the RIGHT Jemima

LESSON 2
WENDY QUILL
QUILL
IS
FULL UP
OF WRONG

I sometimes feel FULL UP of wrong

Unless you are 'gifted and talented' (like Sophia Nowitsky), it is tricky not to get **FULL UP OF WRONG**. Especially when you break grown-up rules completely by accident. And everybody breaks them sometimes because they're not really very well made. Here's a list to show you what I mean:

Sophia Nowitsky doesn't

A LIST OF QUITE BADLY-MADE RULES
BY GROWN-UPS

Do invisible dogs count?

♥ *Never* run in corridors but always be on time.

♥ *Always* be kind to animals but never stroke dogs you don't know.

♥ *Never* talk with your mouth full but always say thank you (straight away).

♥ *Never* talk to strangers but *always* be polite.

♥ *Always* tell the truth and *never* lie.

Now, here are some wondering questions: *How* can you *ALWAYS* be polite' to strangers when you're 'not allowed to talk' to them? And *how* can you *ALWAYS* be on time' when you're 'not allowed to run'?

52

You see? They completely don't make sense. Grandad (who knows everything and even wears a hearing aid) says that

'RULES ARE THERE TO BE BROKEN'

—but that must have been in the olden days when everything was black and white. Because now that everything's in colour, breaking the rules gets you into lots of trouble. I know because I actually

found out. It happened when I told a
Slightly Dreadful Lie by accident and
went to play with the wrong Jemima
in completely the WRONG house.

I didn't even know I'd told a Slightly
Dreadful Lie at first. Not until I'd heard
about the fire. You see, Mr Hucclecoate
(our poorly headmaster) was at
home with a sniffly nose so Miss
Pinch was doing assembly—and Miss
Pinch LOVeS doing
assembly because she
gets to tell everybody
off ALL AT ONCE:

Miss Pinch
is always
telling
everyone
off . . .

all . . .

over the . . .

'It has come to my attention that *some of you* have been telling porky pies! I don't wish to mention any names but . . .

She peered over her glasses and stared at Tyler Ainsworth,

. . . it is *not* acceptable to claim that your dog ate your homework when you do not in fact own a dog.'

place . . .

Tyler Ainsworth sniggered because his homework ⸺ALWAYS⸺ gets eaten by dogs (even though he doesn't actually have one).

'Good girl,' I whispered softly, stroking Bathilda Brown's head.

This is how to stroke an invisible head

A HAPPY LITTLE DOG THOUGHT

I'm glad I own a dog. And I'm glad that she's invisible. Invisible dogs NEVER eat homework. (And invisible poos NEVER smell!)

Miss Pinch carried on 'telling us off' because she's very good at it:

'*Neither* is it acceptable to say that you're late for school because "the school bus didn't turn up." As we all know, there is no school bus. And as such, it will *never* turn up.'

Miss Pinch is still telling off!

Tyler Ainsworth sniggered again and had to go and sit at the back. (He's *always* missing school buses that don't actually exist.) Then, after singing very LOUDLY about 'all creatures great and small', Miss Pinch read us a really famous poem that NOBODY had ever

Tyler Ainsworth seems to quite like it

57

heard of. I can't remember it completely, but I think it started EXACTLY like this:

Matilda told Dreadful Lies all of the time,
It made you gasp and stretch in line

I was really enjoying all the Stretching and Gasping (because Miss Pinch doesn't normally do funny poems) when all of a sudden, it was like a NIGHTMARE!

Because she couldn't help shouting: 'Fire!'
People thought she was a bit of a LIAR
That's why, when her Aunt came back from town
Matilda and her house were all BURNT DOWN!!!

Everyone in the hall went as quiet as mice—even Tyler Ainsworth! But I don't think Miss Pinch really truly noticed.

We gasped

We stretched

We went quiet as mice

'Don't forget children, Cookery Club has been cancelled due to a Health and Safety Issue with the spoons. Now off you go—single file nicely back to class.'

Miss Pinch *still* hasn't finished!

It's hard to 'single file nicely back to class' when you're thinking about fires and things. So we shuffled out in a bumpetty way and got stuck in a lump near the door.

'Florence Hubert,' I whispered, noisily, 'Did you hear what Miss Pinch actually said? Matilda and her house got burnt!'

'I know, Wendy Quill!' said Florence
Hubert. 'I didn't even think it was allowed!'

Suddenly, Sophia Nowitsky interrupted
(because 'gifted and talented' people always
do): 'It was just a "Cautionary Tale",
Wendy Quill. Matilda didn't get
burnt in REAL LIFE. Miss Pinch
was just trying to teach us a lesson.'

'Well, I don't think
it was a very nice sort of
lesson,' I said, shuffling into
the corridor.

Henna
Hussein was
sitting in the

Here we are:
shuffling all
professionally

Library Corner, reading a book about bees. (You're allowed to do that if you've just been to the dentist and things.)

'Hi, Henna Hussein,' I said, nicely.

'Hi, Wendy Quill,' Henna Hussein said back.

A fresh and minty Henna Hussein

(She smelt all fresh and minty because of the gargle and spit.)

SOME FACTS ABOUT HENNA HUSSEIN

Henna Hussein's words are smaller than everybody else's because she's a small-word sort of person. But the rest of her is actually normal size.

Henna Hussein being normal size

'What did I miss?' she asked.

'You missed an IMPORTANT LESSON,' said Sophia Nowitsky, 'about ⟵ALWAYS⟶ telling the truth.'

A Little Wonder: why don't doctors give stickers?

'Oh, I always tell the truth,' said Henna Hussein, fiddling with her 'Keep Smiling' sticker.

'Me too,' Jemima Topps smiled, walking past us (but not running) in the corridor.

We all looked at each other and gasped!

'Did you actually see that!' I said.

Jemima Topps breaking 'girly gang' rules!

'Yes!' Florence Hubert almost squealed. 'Jemima Topps just spoke to us and smiled!'

'And we're not even in the "girly gang"!' Henna Hussein sighed.

SOME GIRLY GANG RULES
(THAT YOU ACTUALLY NEED TO KNOW OR THE LAST BIT WON'T MAKE SENSE)

♥ You must ᷄always᷄ wear earrings.

♥ You must ᷄always᷄ wear pointy shoes.

♥ You must ᷄never᷄ get your clothes dirty.

♥ You must ᷄never᷄ be nice to, or smile at, non-GIRLY GANG MEMBERS (even if they live just over the road).

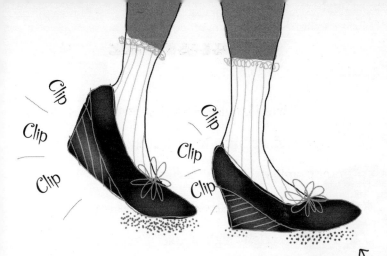

I watched Jemima Topps go clippetting
into class and remembered one of my
yesterdays. Suddenly, I felt **FULL UP OF WRONG!**

It is quite hard not being jealous of clippetty shoes

'What's the matter, Wendy Quill?'
asked Florence Hubert.

'I think I might have told a Slightly
Dreadful Lie!'

'What?!' Florence Hubert gasped. 'Like
Matilda?!!! But her house got completely
burnt down!'

65

'I know!' I gasped back.

'It's *just* a poem,' said Sophia Nowitsky. 'It didn't *really* happen!'

'Well, even if Matilda just got coughy with smoke, it's still really, really bad,' said Florence Hubert.

Sophia Nowitsky huffed off to her desk.

'What Slightly Dreadful Lie did you actually tell, Wendy Quill?' asked Henna Hussein, still smelling all fresh.

I chewed my lip in a worrative way. I didn't actually really want to talk about it. Not even to my very best friends. But Grandad says:

Sophia Nowitsky is quite good at huffing

66

'a trouble shared is a trouble halved.'

So I decided to spread it all out. 'Well,' I whispered, hushatively. 'Mum gave me some HOME-MADE STICKY FLAPJACKS to take to Jemima Topps' house (because you "should ALWAYS be nice to neighbours" and she lives just over the road). But Jemima Topps is in the "girly gang" and they have really mean rules. So I took the HOME-MADE

Sticky flapjacks

This is the RIGHT Jemima

Sticky
flapjacks

STICKY FLAPJACKS to Jemima

Button's house instead. She giggles and

has lots of fluffy gerbils.'

'That's not a *Dreadful Lie*, Wendy

Quill,' said Florence Hubert, not getting it

at all. 'You **LOVE** giggles and gerbils.'

'But Florence Hubert,' I said, 'when

Mum asked: "Did you have a nice time at

Jemima's house?" I just said: "YES!"'

'So? You *were* at a Jemima's house. And you *did*

give her sticky flapjacks. What's *not true* about that?'

'She was at the WRONG house with

the WRONG Jemima!' sneered Angelina

Hardthorpe (who wasn't supposed to be

listening at all).

Ha Ha
Ha Ha

This is the
WRONG Jemima
(who giggles a lot)

'So she LIED. Just like Matilda. And *I'm* going to tell Jemima Topps!'

* This is just a little sad and empty space so you know how full of wrong I actually felt. sigh*

Angelina Hardthorpe is VERY good at hurting feelings

'Florence Hubert,' I sighed, opening my spelling book: 'What *am* I going to do? If Angelina Hardthorpe tells Jemima Topps that I went to COMPLETELY THE WRONG HOUSE, she will probably hate me FOREVER.'

'No she won't,' said Florence Hubert, kindly, 'she will only hate you for a little bit.'

'Oh,' I said, not really feeling better.

My name is Jemima Topps!

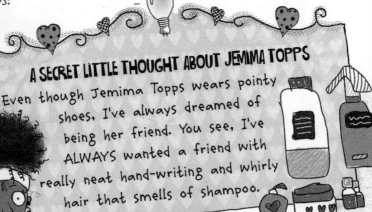

A SECRET LITTLE THOUGHT ABOUT JEMIMA TOPPS

Even though Jemima Topps wears pointy shoes, I've always dreamed of being her friend. You see, I've ALWAYS wanted a friend with really neat hand-writing and whirly hair that smells of shampoo.

I stood up to have a peek. Maybe
Angelina Hardthorpe *wouldn't* actually tell
on me?

Maybe she was too busy trying to get 10 out of 10?

She was getting out her glittery pink pencil case.

She was leaning over the desk.

She was . . .

'SIT DOWN, WENDY QUILL!'

said Miss Pinch.

I'm normally really good at spelling. I can even spell IGUANA and DOUBT. But it's hard to concentrate when you're waiting to be told on. And waiting to be told on is worse than swimming in the deep end when you can't. That's why I couldn't remember any triangle names in Maths and kept dropping my hoop in PE!

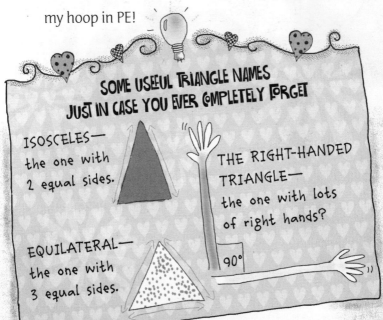

SOME USEFUL TRIANGLE NAMES
JUST IN CASE YOU EVER COMPLETELY FORGET

ISOSCELES—
the one with
2 equal sides.

THE RIGHT-HANDED
TRIANGLE—
the one with lots
of right hands?

EQUILATERAL—
the one with
3 equal sides.

90°

At last, when we were in the changing rooms for PE, I saw Angelina Hardthorpe whispering into one of Jemima Topps' pierced ears. I hid behind the pegs and wished I could completely disappear.

This is my 'wishing hard' face

In two or maybe four minutes, Jemima Topps would know EVERYTHING! And then she would NEVER be my friend.

I waited for the bell. But it takes quite a long time when you're waiting . . . especially when your watch doesn't work.

Suddenly, the bell DRINGLED and I ran outside

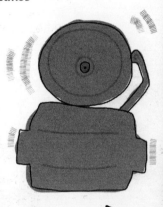

as fast as I could. But they were both already there, waiting in their skirts and pointy shoes.

'Hey, Wendy Quill,' Angelina Hardthorpe sneered. 'I've told Jemima Topps about how you LIED and gave

AN ACTUAL DRAWING FACT: it is not easy to draw 'dringle' noises

75

FACT: telling the truth
is even harder than
drawing dringle noises

ALL the STICKY FLAPJACKS to the
WRONG Jemima in completely the
WRONG house.'

I smiled in a 'SORRY' sort of way.

'Why didn't you come to my house,
Wendy Quill?' asked Jemima Topps. 'I only
live over the road.'

'Yeah,' said Angelina Hardthorpe,
like a really mean echo. 'Why didn't you,
Wendy Quill?'

I looked at Bathilda Brown. She
dribbled on my knee like a friend. It
actually made me feel brave: 'The real truth
is . . . ' I said, remembering what happens
when you lie, 'Jemima Button giggles all

Bathilda Brown
always dribbles
when she's happy

77

the time and has lots of fluffy gerbils. And she's *not* in the "girly gang" so she's always really nice to me.'

'That is totally *tragic*,' said Angelina Hardthorpe (because I think she'd heard it on TV).

But Jemima Topps just looked sad.

'Come on, Jemima Topps,' laughed Angelina Hardthorpe. 'Wendy Quill's not even in our gang.'

When I got home, I told Mum EVERYTHING. About upsetting Jemima

Angelina Hardthorpe has a really professional sneer

78

Topps, about going to the WRONG
house (all full of the WRONG Jemima),
and about telling a Slightly Dreadful Lie
completely by accident.

'Well, goodness me!' said Mum,
'What on earth were you thinking?'

'That I was at a JEMIMA'S HOUSE.
So I was sort of doing as I was told.'

Mum always
cleans the
table when
she's worried
or cross

Sticky
flapjacks

'No you weren't!' said Mum. 'You were giving STICKY FLAPJACKS to the WRONG Jemima in the WRONG HOUSE! What if I'd sent Woody to find you and you weren't even there! How do you think I'd have felt?'

WRONG
Jemima

'YOU'D HAVE FELT ALL FULL UP OF WORRY.'

I said. 'And Dad would have been on the news. And people would have been looking for me with torches in the dark! And it

WRONG
house

This is COMPLETELY the wrong house!

would have been really *awful*!!!' I almost-nearly cried!

'Well, maybe not quite that bad,' said Mum. 'But I do need to know where you are.'

'I'm ever so sorry,' I said, looking around. (I needed to stroke Bathilda Brown but she wasn't even there!)

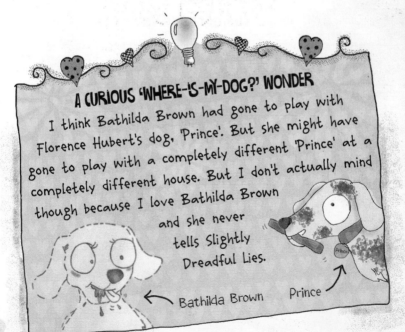

A CURIOUS 'WHERE-IS-MY-DOG?' WONDER

I think Bathilda Brown had gone to play with Florence Hubert's dog, 'Prince'. But she might have gone to play with a completely different 'Prince' at a completely different house. But I don't actually mind though because I love Bathilda Brown and she never tells Slightly Dreadful Lies.

← Bathilda Brown   Prince

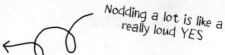

Nodding a lot is like a really loud YES

'Just promise me you'll *always* tell the truth,' said Mum.

I nodded lots and lots of times. 'I really do promise that I will NEVER tell a lie to ANYONE again. Even if it is by accident. And I'll definitely NEVER go to see the wrong Jemima in the completely wrong house *ever again*.'

'Good,' Mum smiled. 'Now, the question is, how are you going to make it up to Jemima Topps?'

'I don't think I actually really can!' Mum passed me some bright yellow butter. 'Of course you can. Just make

82

some *more* STICKY FLAPJACKS all by yourself. But for the RIGHT Jemima Topps this time.'

A VERY IMPORTANT 'MUST-READ' NOTE

Dear very-friendly and extremely-nice reader

STICKY FLAPJACKS take quite a long time to cook, so can you please look the other way or go to the toilet while I try my very bestest not to burn them.

Thank you very much

Lots of love from

Wendy Quill

xx

Jemima Topps' house is just in front of our house but sort of higher up and looking down. So I crossed the road (very carefully—just like PC Lacey said)

My tummy felt all nervous and gurgly . . .

and hop-skotched up the steps. Then, I knocked on the bright green front door. At first, I thought nobody was in. But suddenly, all of Jemima Topps was there! She had changed into a sparkly love-heart dress with completely matching tights and had three brand-new red streaks in her hair!

'Hello Jemima Topps,' I grinned, trying very hard to be her friend. 'I **LOVE** the new bits in your hair!'

... until Jemima Topps opened the door

'Thank you, Wendy Quill,' she smiled back (even though she's not supposed to).

85

'My mum just did it. It takes *ages* to wash out. Even when you use shampoo.'

'Wow,' I sniffed. 'I don't think I told you. I _LOVE_ the smell of your hair.'

PLEASE SNIFF JEMIMA TOPPS' HAIR HERE!!!

'Thank you, Wendy Quill.' Jemima Topps blushed. 'Your hair smells quite nice too.'

'Oh, mine's just a special shampoo that keeps the nits away.'

'Have you got nits?' asked Jemima Topps, curiously.

'No,' I sighed, 'I'm not actually allowed them. I mean, I did have them for a little bit. But Mum doesn't like things that

86

poo in the house or even in people's hair.
So she combed them all out and threw
them down the toilet, which was a little bit
like a nightmare. Especially when you want
to be a vet. But Woody says they can swim
so I think they're actually okay.'

'Oh,' giggled Jemima Topps. I giggled
back (because trying-to-be-friends was
going very well).

'Do you want some HOME MADE
STICKY FLAPJACKS?' I asked, passing

her my red, spotty
plate. 'I made
it all by
myself.'

A very
sticky way
to make
friends

87

'Yes please,' smiled Jemima Topps.

'Wendy Quill, would you like to come in?'

I grinned and stepped into the

RIGHT house.

Jemima Topps' kitchen isn't like *our*

kitchen. It doesn't have saucepans in the

sink. In fact, it's all sparkly and white.

'I **LOVE** your kitchen, Jemima Topps,' I said. 'Is it always this empty and clean?'

'Mmmf,' Jemima Topps chewed, which means 'yes' when your mouth is really full. 'This is the BEST FLAPJACK I've ever tasted. It's even getting stuck on my teeth!'

I LOVE having sticky teeth in common!

'It gets stuck on mine too!' I said. 'It's great that we have such a lot in common!'

Jemima Topps giggled (again!)

and gave me an ENORMOUS piece.

'Do you want to come and see my room?'

'Mmmf,' I said (which still means

'yes' when your mouth is really full). So we

went upstairs and stood outside a door.

It said:

This is JEMIMA'S bedroom

'Wow!' I sighed. 'I **LOVE** things

with names on them. I've actually got

two T-shirts with my name on

them. That's why no-

one forgets who I am.'

Wendy is a Little Princess

Wendy is a Little Star

Get a T-shirt with your name on so NO-ONE forgets who you are

'I know, *Wendy Quill*,' Jemima Topps winked, making a very good joke. 'You see, your T-shirts really do work.'

She opened her bedroom door:

'WOW!' I cried. 'Your bedroom's AMAZING! It's ever so much BIGGER

Look!
A bedroom
that's NOT
even shared

than mine. And I LOVE the way you're not sharing it.'

Woody

'Thanks,' said Jemima Topps. 'But actually, if I tell you the complete truth, I feel a bit all on my own.'

'Really?' I asked, full of surprise.

'Yes,' said Jemima Topps, 'The *real* truth is: I wish I had a sister and a brother like you. But Dad says they cost too much money.'

'No they don't,' I said, saying a fact. 'Woody and Tawny were free.'

Jemima Topps giggled again (even though she doesn't at school). Then she sat down in front of her mirror. 'Can I ask you

Tawny

Completely free.
Ta daa!

92

something?' she asked, playing with one of
her whirls.

'Of course you can,' I said. 'As long as
it's not a question with a right answer. Like:
what's the capital of Switzerland? Or: how
far is it to Timbuktu? I'm not very good
at those. I'm much better at *wondering
questions*. Like: are camels proud of their
humps? Or: what is the silliest fruit?'

'What *is* the silliest fruit?!' asked
Jemima Topps, curiously.

'Well, when I was little, I thought
it was a pineapple—because of the
spikiness and bits at the top. And bananas
are quite funny because of the bend.

*Jemima
Topps' hair
whirls all
over the
place*

93

But then Grandad brought an African

cucumber at the market which made

me *giggle-wheeze* until I couldn't

actually stop. So the African cucumber is

definitely the silliest fruit. Is that what you

wanted to ask?'

'Erm. No. Not exactly.'

'Well, was it a

wondering sort of question?'

'No. Not really.' She took a deep

breath. 'I just wanted to know if Angelina

Hardthorpe was telling the truth.'

'About what?' I nervously asked.

'About you having an invisible dog.

You know. Called Bathilda Brown?'

My very
favourite,
silliest fruit

94

'Oh yes, that's true,' I beamed
(because I knew the answer already).

Invisible dogs quite like sleeping

'In fact, she's asleep on your bed.'

'Is she?' Jemima Topps turned around
to look.

'Yes. Sorry about the invisible dog
hairs. They get EVERYWHERE all of

95

the time.' I brushed them off with my hand. 'Wake up, Bathilda Brown. It's time for your walk.' Then, I patted my leg like a real professional dog walker and Bathilda Brown completely woke up. 'Shall we call on Florence Hubert and take her down the brook?' I asked. 'She **LOVES** getting muddy with Prince.'

Bathilda Brown completely waking up

'BARK!'

barked Bathilda Brown (all invisibly).

'Oh, I *can't*,' sighed Jemima Topps. '"Girly gang" members aren't allowed to get their clothes or shoes mucky. It's one of Angelina Hardthorpe's rules.'

'That's awful!' I said, because it really was. Suddenly, I had an AMAZING IDEA that popped into my head like a dream. 'You can come round to my house and wear MY clothes. Then you can get muddy all over and it won't actually count! I've even got a spare pair of AMAZING sensible shoes!'

My beautiful, invisible, dribbly dog . . . barking invisibly

This is my first ever jumpy-up-and-down hug with Jemima Topps!

'Really? Do you mean it, Wendy Quill?' asked Jemima Topps, suddenly squeezing me tight!

'Yes, I really do,' I squeezed back.

LESSON 2

Only a little bit later (I don't know exactly how much later because of my slightly-broken-even-though-I-still-love-it watch), Florence Hubert, Jemima Topps, Prince, Bathilda Brown, and me were getting slightly soggy down the brook.

'I'm really sorry about going to the WRONG house,' I said to Jemima Topps. 'I'll NEVER do it again. Pinky Promise.'

'I know you won't,' grinned Jemima Topps, putting her little finger through mine.

You must always love your slightly-broken watch

Pinky promises are actually for life

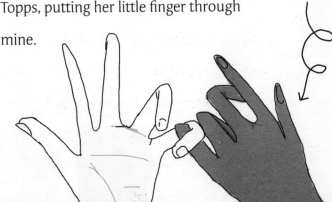

LESSON 2

'You actually look really nice in Wendy
Quill's clothes,' said Florence Hubert, being
Jemima Topps' friend too. (Jemima Topps
was wearing my best stripy leggings, a
green flowery T-shirt and my old pair of
AMAZING SENSIBLE SHOES.)

The
specialest
shoe in the
world!!!

'Thank you, Florence Hubert,' said
Jemima Topps. 'I've actually always loved
Wendy Quill's style.'

'What style?' I asked,
because I didn't really have one.

'Your style of "things-that-
don't-match",' said Jemima Topps.

I looked at my leggings in surprise.
Then, I *giggle-wheezed* completely
by accident!

They love my style
of 'THINGS-THAT-
DON'T-MATCH'

giggle-wheeze

giggle-wheeze

wheeze

giggle-wheeze

giggle

ze

giggle-wheeze

ze

giggle

giggle-

wheeze

giggle-wheeze

giggle-wheeze

giggle-wh

wheeze

gigg

giggle-wheeze

giggle-wheeze

heeze

giggle-wheeze

giggle-wheeze

gig

'You're actually completely right, Jemima Topps!' said Florence Hubert. 'I **LOVE** Wendy Quill's "things-that-don't-match" style too.'

Florence Hubert —doing AMAZING things with her hands!!!

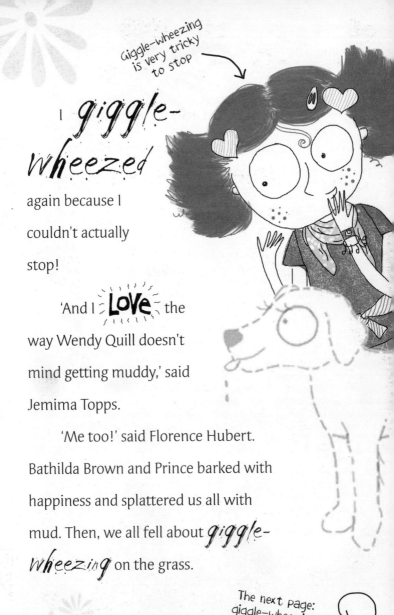

Giggle-wheezing is very tricky to stop

I **giggle-wheezed** again because I couldn't actually stop!

'And I **LOVE** the way Wendy Quill doesn't mind getting muddy,' said Jemima Topps.

'Me too!' said Florence Hubert. Bathilda Brown and Prince barked with happiness and splattered us all with mud. Then, we all fell about *giggle-wheezing* on the grass.

The next page: giggle-wheezing all over the place!

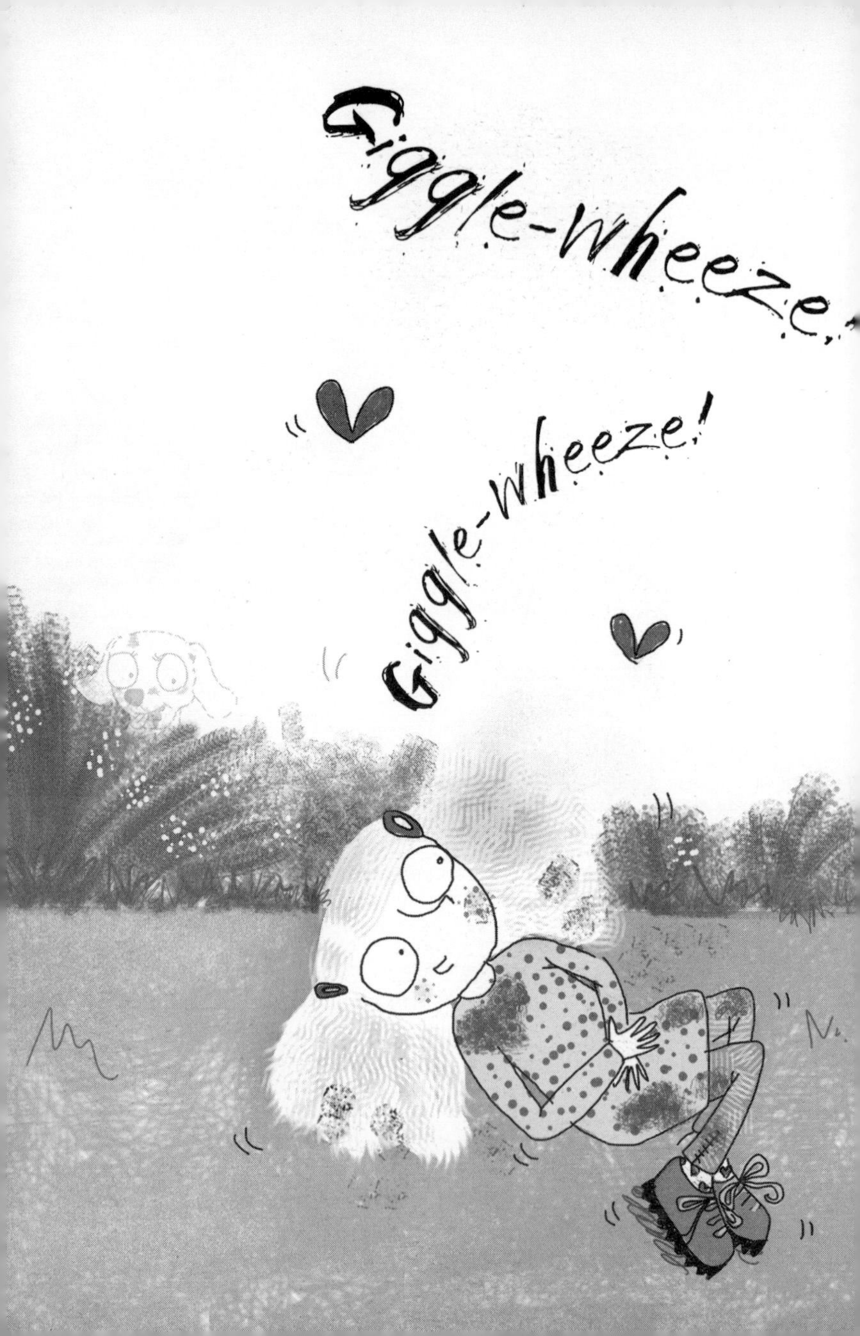
Giggle-wheeze.
Giggle-wheeze!

My new friend Jemima Topps, has nearly learnt how to giggle-wheeze ←

'Wendy Quill,'

Jemima Topps

laughed, all out of breath.

'I don't think I actually want to be in

the "GIRLY GANG" any more. Can I

be in your gang instead?'

'That would be very lovely, Jemima Topps,'

I said. 'But I don't actually have a GANG.

I've just got lots of nice friends instead.'

'Aw, thanks Wendy Quill,' Florence

Hubert grinned.

'BARK,'

'BARK,' barked

Bathilda Brown

and Prince.

← I am actually very good at it already

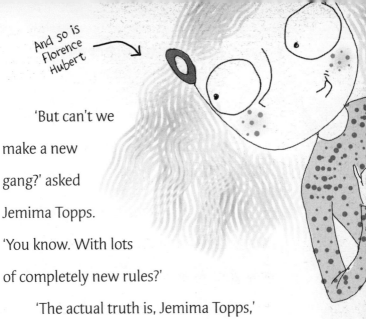

And so is Florence Hubert

'But can't we make a new gang?' asked Jemima Topps. 'You know. With lots of completely new rules?'

'The actual truth is, Jemima Topps,' I said. 'I'm not really sure about gangs.'

'Why not?' asked Jemima Topps.

'Well, they just always leave people out.'

'Yes, but what if we have an AMAZING GANG where everybody's actually allowed in?'

Prince and Bathilda Brown can't really giggle-wheeze yet. But that's because they're dogs

'Oh, that would be really quite nice,'
I said (because it really would).

'What shall we call it, Wendy Quill?'
asked Florence Hubert. I squeezed my eyes
and thought about it hard: 'What about the
Giggle-Wheeze Gang?'
I asked, suddenly clapping my hands.

'That is BRILLIANT!' said Florence
Hubert. 'You are always *giggle-wheezing*,
Wendy Quill. In fact, you never really stop.'

YOU can
be in my
GIGGLE-
WHEEZE
GANG if
you like

'I do if I think about poorly cats,' I said, because that was an actual fact.

'Poorly cats?' asked Jemima Topps, curiously.

'Yes. It's one of our Special Secret Tricks.'

'WOW!' sighed Jemima Topps happily. 'I completely LOVE Special Secret Tricks.'

My Special Secret Trick to stop me giggle-wheezing

THE VERY IMPORTANT MORAL OF THIS STORY
Try not to go to the WRONG house when you're meant to be at the RIGHT one.

PS: If you would actually like to join our Giggle-Wheeze Gang, please just look at our TOP SECRET rules at the back!

LESSON 3

WENDY ♥ QUILL

AND THE DIARY THAT WOULDN'T STAY SHUT

A secret: this chapter might actually be haunted!

Everybody has secrets. Even invisible dogs.

And most of them are really exciting and

completely not known. You've probably

got hundreds and lots. Some are big

and some are small, but mine are mostly

sort of in-between. But when you

start turning into a teenager, they

grow and won't all fit inside your

small secret

in-between secret

big secret

Teenagers are full up of these!!!

head. That's why you have to start writing them down. I know because my big sister Tawny actually does it every night. When she thinks that no one's looking, she writes them all down in her **TOTALLY PRIVATE DIARY** and puts it on the CAN'T REACH SHELF.

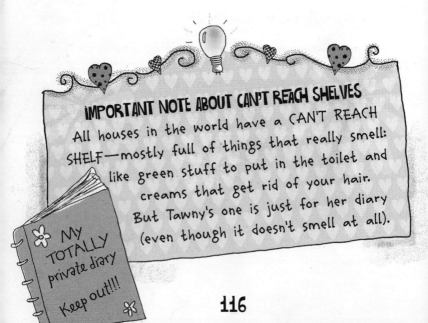

IMPORTANT NOTE ABOUT CAN'T REACH SHELVES
All houses in the world have a CAN'T REACH SHELF—mostly full of things that really smell: like green stuff to put in the toilet and creams that get rid of your hair.
But Tawny's one is just for her diary (even though it doesn't smell at all).

My TOTALLY private diary Keep out!!!

I've got a CAN'T REACH SHELF in
my bedroom—but it's on TAWNY'S
SIDE of the room. I don't really
know who put it there, but it's
been there for hundreds
of years (even though our
house is quite new). I used to
really wish it was on MY SIDE—
and Florence Hubert wanted one too. But
we don't any more. Not now we know
about the ghost.

I didn't actually believe in ghosts until the
cracketty storm. I mean, I sort of believed
in Jemima Topps' tooth fairy, but that's

*I am completely
not reaching*

117

only because she's called Gossamer Dew

and actually writes back all the time.

And invisible dogs are definitely true

because I've got one all of my own.

But I thought ghosts were just in stories.

Or grown-ups pretending with sheets.

I didn't know they actually existed.

Especially not in my room!

Anyway, because it was a Saturday

and there was lots of wet rain and

cracketty bits of thunder, Florence

Hubert and me were upstairs

playing on MY SIDE of the

room. We were busy doing

exciting things because 'only

A little wonder: where do tooth fairies live?

Tut Tut Tut

That should be "I" not "me"!

boring children

get bored'—like wrapping each

other up in toilet paper (just like

real Egyptians used to do).

I LOVE turning into an Egyptian Mummy

AN INTERESTING FACT ABOUT EGYPTIAN TOILETS

Even though Florence Hubert thought Egyptians invented toilet paper (because they needed lots to wrap up all the Mummies), Woody says they actually did not. In his Encyclopaedia, it says that the Chinese invented toilet paper in 500 AD. So that means the Egyptians didn't actually have any toilet paper! But they definitely invented toilet seats—so at least they could sit down while they were waiting.

Careful
somersaults
are best

Anyway, the toilet paper had all run
out so we started doing somersaults on
my bed. (It's important to practice if you
want to be a professional but you have to

be careful because of the springs.) Anyway,

that's when Florence Hubert noticed

Tawny's **TOTALLY PRIVATE DIARY**—sitting

all on its own.

'Wendy Quill,' she asked, all of a sudden.

'What's that book doing all up on high?'

She was looking at the

CAN'T REACH SHELF.

'Oh,' I said, very

wisely (because I

actually knew).

'That is Tawny's

TOTALLY

PRIVATE DIARY.

She writes in it

every night.'

Florence
Hubert is
pointing
really well

↙

'Why?' asked Florence

Hubert, because she doesn't

have a big sister yet.

'So that her head doesn't get too full

of secrets,' I whispered. 'It's just

what *all* teenagers do.'

1 secret

2 secrets

3 secrets

4 secrets

5 secrets

6 secrets

7 secrets

8 secrets

'Wow!' Florence

Hubert sighed. 'I wish

I was already a teenager.'

'I don't think I actually do,' I said.

'Why not?' asked Florence Hubert,

curiously. I ran to my SPECIAL DRAWER

Teenagers'
heads get
quite full

and got out my BEST SPOTTY NOTEBOOK.

'Because of this,' I very nicely said.

LESSON 3

1) Teenagers start to smell quite a lot and spray bottles under their arms.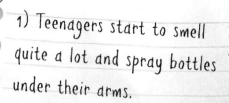

2) Teenagers grow lots of tiny spots. Mostly all over their chins.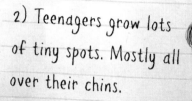

3) Teenagers have to slam doors all the time and it can actually get quite tiring.

4) Teenagers need to huff really well and sometimes forget how to grin! *Huff!*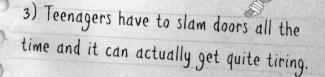

5) Teenagers get lots of homework (and it makes them all flustered and pink).

'That *is* quite tricky,' said Florence Hubert. 'But can I please write a list of my own?'

'Of course you can,' I smiled. 'That is what best friends are for. You can even use my BEST SPOTTY NOTEBOOK. And my very own Lucky Brownish Pen!'

Everybody should have one of these

'Gosh! Thank you, Wendy Quill,' said Florence Hubert (knowing just how special they are). Then, this is what she actually wrote down:

A LIST OF REASONS WHY I WOULD LIKE TO BE ALREADY A TEENAGER, BY FLORENCE HUBERT

1) Teenagers are allowed to use grown up shampoo and put special stuff on their hair.

2) Teenagers are allowed to go out with their friends and buy strawberry milkshakes in town.

3) Teenagers can wear black nail varnish and never have to take it all off.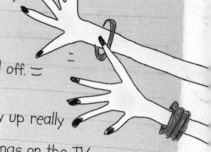

4) Teenagers get to stay up really late and watch scary things on the TV.

5) Teenagers have REALLY BIG SECRETS and PRIVATE DIARIES all of their own!

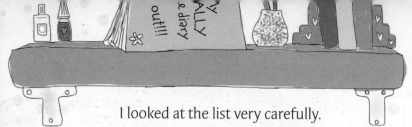

I looked at the list very carefully.

'I think you are right, Florence Hubert.'
I said. 'Being a teenager's nice!'

We both stared at the CAN'T
REACH SHELF. Tawny's diary was
completely still there!

The
TOTALLY
PRIVATE
DIARY
not moving

'Wendy Quill,' asked Florence Hubert.
'What sort of secrets do you think Tawny
actually keeps?'

'I'm not exactly sure, Florence Hubert,'
I said. 'But they're definitely really quite
BIG.'

'Bigger than mine and Laurence's?'
asked Florence Hubert, curiously.

'Much bigger than *that*!' I grinned.

128

Florence Hubert and Laurence Hubert's aunty gives them really sticky lollipops every time they go there for their tea. That's because she works in a sweet shop. But they don't tell Ms Hubert because she doesn't really like that sort of thing.

We stared at the CAN'T REACH

SHELF again.

'Wendy Quill,' said Florence Hubert.

'Because I go to Scouts every Thursday,

I have to *always be prepared*. It is one of

our "Important Scout Rules". And I would

really like to be prepared for being a

teenager. So can I have a little look? Just to

check how big they actually are?'

'OF COURSE NOT!'

I gasped, all full of surprise. 'That would be almost quite SNEAKY!'

'Oh. I'm sorry, Wendy Quill,' said Florence Hubert (because she didn't even realize it at all). Suddenly, there was an

ENORMOUS

CRACKETY

and the lights did a bit of sudden flick!

'Gosh!' Florence Hubert giggled, jumping out of her skin (which is actually just a saying and not true). 'I'm soooo glad we're *not* outside.'

FLASH!

'Me too!' I said, peering out of the window. 'And I hope Benjamina's okay.

When she's nervous, she starts pooing everywhere—especially in storms!'

'Don't worry,' said Florence Hubert. 'At least she's got a really snuggly hutch. What about Socrates? Is he still outside?'

AN IMPORTANT FACT ABOUT SOCRATES

'Socrates' is actually my big whiskery cat and not a really famous dead old man from Greece (you know, the philosophery one who was always asking questions with a beard). That Socrates was definitely not outside—even though my cat was named after his whiskers.

This is Socrates (my cat) trying to look like Socrates (the philosopher)

'Socrates is hiding in the airing cupboard,' I said.

'What? All on his own?' asked Florence Hubert.

'Of course not,' I answered back. 'He's hiding with Bathilda Brown.'

'Oh, that's all right then,' said Florence Hubert, all shruggy with relief. 'But what shall we actually do now? I can't stop thinking about teenagers and things.'

We looked at the CAN'T REACH SHELF again. The **TOTALLY PRIVATE DIARY** was *still* there. Florence Hubert sighed.

'I know,' I said. 'Maybe we *could* practise our somersaults on *Tawny's* bed. I think it might have some

The TOTALLY PRIVATE DIARY STILL not moving

133

EXTRA BOUNCE?'

'Okay,' Florence Hubert grinned. 'But is it completely allowed?'

'Not completely.' I looked at Tawny's SIDE. 'But Tawny goes to Romilly Pucker's every Saturday. So I'm sure that she wouldn't really mind.'

I am actually quite good at bouncing

'Brilliant,' said Florence Hubert,
looking at the CAN'T REACH SHELF again.
'Why don't we do star jumps instead?'

'What? With our arms stretched out
like this?' I asked, bouncing and doing my
very widest stretch.

'Yes! Just like that!' Florence Hubert
nodded.

'But what if we knock something off?'
I asked. 'You know, off the CAN'T REACH
SHELF?'

'Then it will only be completely by
accident,' said Florence Hubert, bouncing
and roly-polying too.

135

The next page:
star jumping and
roly-polying like
professionals!!!

My TOTALLY private diary

Keep out!!!

I LOVE it when things nearly wobble off!

Star jumping on squishy beds is actually quite tiring. But we both did it really, really well. Florence Hubert went much higher than me, but I'm actually better at spreading out. That's why it was MY hand that touched the CAN'T REACH SHELF completely by accident first.

'Oh no, Florence Hubert!' I gasped. 'The diary's almost slightly wobbling off!'

'Oh no!' Florence Hubert gasped too. But . . . it didn't.

'Try again!' said Florence Hubert.

I stretched my very best star jump . . . but it still just wobbled on the edge.

138

'Again! Again!' said Florence Hubert,

almost sort of clapping!

Dad doesn't normally wear binoculars inside

'WHAT ON EARTH ARE YOU DOING UP THERE?'

shouted Dad, quite loudly through

the floor. 'You sound like a

stampeding herd of elephants!'

'SORRY,' we both shouted

back. Then, we flopped on Tawny's

bed and sighed. (Star jumping is

VERY hard work.)

'I am actually quite glad that Tawny's **TOTALLY PRIVATE DIARY** didn't fall off by accident,' I said, gazing at the CAN'T REACH SHELF.

'Why?' asked Florence Hubert, like a question.

'Because teenage secrets *are* secret. And if we accidentally read them, then they sort of wouldn't be secret any more.'

'I suppose you are right, Wendy Quill. But I only wanted to know what they looked like so I can "*always be prepared*".'

'Never mind,' I said to Florence Hubert, nicely.

Please, please, please, please wobble off!

Lightening is actually quite frightening →

'You've got ages to find out. I mean, we'll be ten one day.'

Suddenly, there was a

GIGANTICALLY ENORMOUS . . .

CRACKETTY FLASH!

. . . that filled up the whole of the room!

'Ahhhhhhhhhhhhhhh'

screamed Florence Hubert.

'Ahhhhhhhhhh!

I screamed back (because it's not girly to

scream if it's an actual real storm).

And *then*, without even star jumping

or anything at all, something AMAZING

happened. Tawny's **TOTALLY PRIVATE**

DIARY fell off the CAN'T REACH SHELF!

Right on top of my fishy leggings!!!

hhhhhh'

And it was completely wide OPEN!

'What happened, Wendy Quill?'

squeaked Florence Hubert.

The wobbling off actually happened!

143

'I don't even know,' I squeaked back.

Florence Hubert stared at the CAN'T REACH SHELF, all full of mystery.

'There's only ONE actual explanation,' she whispered.

The almost-empty Can't Reach Shelf

'What, Florence Hubert?' I asked.

'Well,' she said very slowly: 'The CAN'T REACH SHELF must have its own ghost!'

Look! An actual ghost!

'A *ghost*! In my room! Are you completely sure?'

'Yes!' said Florence Hubert. 'A real and actual ghost! I actually watched a programme all about it. They're called "poltergeists" and they throw things about!

Like diaries and old shoes and plates. You know, because they *want* something.'

'Gosh, Florence Hubert,' I said. 'Thank goodness it's on Tawny's SIDE. What do you think the ghost actually wants?'

'Well,' said Florence Hubert, like a detective. 'If the ghost knocked the diary off the CAN'T REACH SHELF and made it open all by itself, then I think it must want us to read it!!! You know, so we can "always be prepared"!'

Look!
Things that are thrown about!

'Of course, Florence Hubert,' I shivered, suddenly feeling spooky and cold. 'Shall we take the diary over to MY SIDE? I think it's less haunted over there.'

We tiptoed across the carpet when, suddenly (again), there was another . . .

CRACKETTY FLASH!

'Quick! Let's hide under my bed!' I shouted. So we scrambled underneath and lay in the dust.

'I think we better have a look,' said Florence Hubert. 'Before the ghost gets all stroppy and cross.'

'Good idea, Florence Hubert,' I said.

R. P.
4
T. Q.

Dear Diary,

It's such an absolute nightmare having too many teeth. I mean, Romilly Pucker's are perfect but mine are all squeezed together at the back and it's so like, totally annoying. And the worse thing is, Mum says I'll probably have to have an actual brace! You know. Completely glued on! And bits of food are going to get stuck in it and everything!!! GROSS!

And it's like, so totally unfair because all the girls in Year 11 are just so AMAZINGLY attractive—and I'm going to be the only one with a METAL MOUTH! And when I sing high notes in choir it's just going to be tragic. So I'll have to keep my mouth shut forever.

And it's going to SOOOO totally ruin my career.

Try not to read this please. (Unless a ghost told you to)

We are just trying to make the ghost happy

'Oh no!' I said. 'That is a really sad secret. I didn't know teenagers had those!'

'But it doesn't even make sense,' said Florence Hubert. 'Your sister is completely BEAUTIFUL and she'd still look like a famous pop star—even with food in her teeth!'

'Thank you, Florence Hubert,' I said. 'I think so too. Unless it was bread or cheese or maybe toffee because that could actually get in the way.'

148

CRACKETTY FLASH!

'Arghhhhhhh!'

We both jumped again and our heads

bumped the bottom of the bed.

A NOTE ABOUT SCOUTS AND STORMS
Even if you're a Scout, it's actually hard to
ALWAYS BE PREPARED for cracketty thunder,
even if you really, really try.

Then, mysteriously (and because of all the jumping and bumping), the diary flipped over . . .

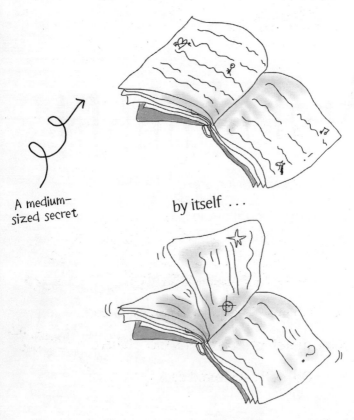

A medium-sized secret

by itself . . .

and landed on a . . .

completely different page!

A really BIG secret

'Oh look! The ghost wants us to read some more!' whispered Florence Hubert.

'Oh yes!' I answered back.

Dear Diary,

I SOOOOOOO hope no-one finds out where I go on Saturday afternoons. All my friends think I go to Romilly Pucker's stables—to help muck out her horse. But I only really do that in the mornings. And if anyone in my form found out that I went to Science Club after lunch, I'd be completely and utterly dead. That's why Mum says I don't have to tell anyone. Everyone would think I'm a complete geek which I soooo am not. Anyway, we made this incredible crystal fountain last week which totally rocked, and today's volcano experiment with Diet Coke and mentos was AWESOME. The Coke was like, EVERYWHERE!!! It even got in my hair!!! Crazy. Can't wait 'til next week.

Mento

Put Mento in Diet Coke

AWESOME!

Here is another page that you probably shouldn't read

'What's wrong with going to Science Club, Wendy Quill?' asked Florence Hubert.

'I don't exactly know,' I said back. 'I'd **LOVE** to do volcano experiments and get Coke in my hair. In fact, I really wish we could go too.'

Wishing we could go to Science Club

'So why doesn't Tawny want her friends to find out? It all seems completely silly.'

Wohooo...
Please read the diary

'I told you that being a teenager was tricky. They're always getting flustered and pink for no reason at all.'

Florence Hubert looked at the diary again. 'I don't think I actually understand teenagers,' she said. 'I mean, it was very nice of the ghost to let us read Tawny's **TOTALLY PRIVATE DIARY**, but I still don't feel very *prepared*. Why would anybody worry about going to really exciting clubs and getting bits stuck in their teeth?'

All full of exciting lists

'Exactly,' I said, grabbing my BEST SPOTTY NOTEBOOK from under the bed and scribbling those down on my list. 'That's why I ⸢**LOVE**⸣ being nine.'

BEST EVER SPOTTY NOTEBOOK

'WENDY QUILL!

FLORENCE HUBERT!'

shouted Mum. 'Come downstairs and have

a little snack.'

'COMING, MUM,' I shouted

back.

'But what about the ghost, Wendy

Quill?' asked Florence Hubert.

'I don't think ghosts eat snacks,' I said.

155

Mum does a very nice wink

Tawny had just rushed in the front door and was sitting at the table already. She was a little bit wet from the storm (or maybe some sort of experiment?).

'Did you have a nice time, Tawny?' Mum winked.

'Yes thanks, Mum,' Tawny winked back.

Florence Hubert winked at me and I winked back because we couldn't actually really help it. But then, we tried very hard

not to look like we knew anything about
Science Club at all!

'What's up with you two?' asked
Tawny. 'You're acting weird.'

'Oh, they're just a bit excited by the
storm,' said Mum.

We both nodded a lot to say 'yes'.

'Whatever,' said Tawny, taking a sip
of her very milky, decaffeinated (so she
doesn't get too over-stimulated) tea.

We are
definitely
trying not to
look weird

157

(We both had elderflower pop.)

'I **LOVE** your teeth,' said Florence Hubert, all suddenly and out of the blue.

'Pardon?' said Tawny.

'She just said that she loved your teeth,' I joined in. 'And actually, so do I. All of them. Even the ones at the back.'

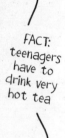

FACT: teenagers have to drink very hot tea

'What?' asked Tawny, all confused.

'All of them. I mean, we **LOVE** all of them. Don't we, Florence Hubert? Even if there's actually quite a lot. And you can't even tell and I don't think it even really matters.'

'It doesn't matter at all, Wendy Quill,' said Florence Hubert. 'Not even when you

open your mouth.' She opened
her mouth very wide.

'And a bit of stuck
flapjack might
actually be quite
nice,' I said, sort
of wiggling my tongue.

'Oh yes,' said Florence Hubert.
'In fact, you could save it for later.'

'What are you two going on
about?' asked Tawny, suspiciously.

'Nothing,' we both sweetly said.

Suddenly, Tawny stood up and ran to
our room. 'I wonder what's got into her?'
said Mum.

Florence
Hubert is a
really good
tongue-
wiggler

ARGHH
HHHHH

Teenagers scream quite a lot

screamed Tawny, running down the stairs.

'Someone's been reading my

TOTALLY PRIVATE DIARY!!!!!!

I found it under *Wheezy Bird's*

bed!!!!!!!'

We both went completely

red—even though we didn't

actually mean to.

'Wendy. Dotterel. Quill!' said Mum.

'Has this got something to do with you?'

'Erm. Sort of. Maybe. Quite,' I said.

Pulling my
very best
'quite' face

'Quite?!'

shrieked Tawny. 'What's that

supposed to mean?'

'*Quite*?' asked Mum.

'Yes,' I said. 'Quite. Because it

was mostly to do with the ghost,' I said.

'What ghost?' shrieked Tawny.

'What ghost?' asked Mum.

'The one that lives on Tawny's side,'
I explained. 'You know, that lives on the
CAN'T REACH SHELF. It threw Tawny's
TOTALLY PRIVATE DIARY on my leggings
in the storm! It's even got a very special
name. Tell them, Florence Hubert.'

Florence Hubert puffed up all proudly.
'They're called "poltergeists" and they're a
SCIENTIFIC FACT. I saw a programme about
them on TV. They throw things about when
they want you to do something—like read
someone's **TOTALLY PRIVATE DIARY** so you
can always be prepared.'

I told you this chapter was a bit haunted . . .

162

Wooooooooo!!!

'But we only read the bits that the ghost showed us,' I said. 'Otherwise it would have been quite rude.'

Tawny's hair gets very drippy when it's wet

'Which bits did you read, Wendy Quill?'

asked Tawny (sounding a bit like Miss Pinch).

'Well, it was mostly about Science Club and your brace,' I said, because you should always tell the truth.

164

'Mum!'

screeched Tawny,

'Do something!'

'All right, all right,' said Mum. 'Tawny,

please calm down. Now, first things

first—Wendy Dotterel Quill: you should

NEVER read someone else's diary.'

'Even if a ghost . . . ?' I began.

'*Even* if a ghost told you to,' said Mum.

'Tell her she can't go down the

brook EVER AGAIN,' squealed Tawny, for

absolutely no reason at all.

165

'No, Tawny,' said Mum. 'I think an apology will suffice.'

'I'm ever so sorry, Tawny,' I said. 'I didn't know you'd be quite so cross.'

'I'm sorry too,' said Florence Hubert (even though she was just a guest). Tawny HUFFED and folded her arms.

'But on reflection,' said Mum, stroking Tawny's wet hair, 'I think we should have told the girls about Science Club.'

'What!' Tawny gasped, all surprised.

'Well, Tawny,' said Mum. 'We haven't been *completely* honest. And we've been telling *Wheezy Bird* that she should *always tell the truth*. Even if it's

Mums are always ever so wise

difficult sometimes. Besides, I think it's time you stood up for yourself. Be proud of who you are. It doesn't really matter what other people think.'

'Of course it does,' said Tawny. 'All my friends will completely hate me.'

'Well, maybe you need to think a little bit about who your friends *really* are?' said Mum.

'I know who they are,' Tawny scowled.

'*Do you*? Do you *really*?' said Mum, all mysteriously. Tawny sipped some more tea.

'Well, they don't sound like very nice friends,' I said. 'And *we* think you're the

Tawny—being a very cool teenager

coolest teenager in the world—especially now we know you go to Science Club.'

'Yes, we really do,' Florence Hubert nodded. 'And we don't even mind about your teeth.'

Us—not even minding about Tawny's teeth

Tawny stared at us. Then, she started to laugh (even though she didn't really want to). Then she gave us both a really

Big sisters do the
best hugs EVER

big hug. Then Mum laughed too (because
hug-watching makes her happy).

'Guys, you're both really brilliant,' said
Tawny. 'But *please* don't *ever* read my diary
again. Even if a ghost tries to make you!!!'

'Of course not, Tawny.' I winked. 'We
don't need to. Not now we're *completely
prepared*!'

MORAL TO LESSON 3
Don't always do what ghosts tell you.
Sometimes, they're not actually right.

THE VERY slightly haunted HAPPY END

EXTRA BITS

THAT ARE A TOTAL SURPRISE

BIT ONE:

WENDY QUILL'S
TOP SECRET RULES
FOR THE
Giggle-Wheeze Gang

Rule 1: **Giggle-wheezers** always smile PROFESSIONALLY.

Practice your very best smile!

Thinking about poorly cats helps!

Jemima Topps looks AMAZING in my best clothes-that-don't-match

Rule 2: You MUST learn how to *Giggle-Wheeze* properly—a little bit like a sea-lion. (But learn our secret trick so you can stop!)

Rule 3: Try to wear some clothes that DON'T match. If you haven't got any of your own, don't worry. Just borrow someone else's.

Rule 4: Make a lot of VERY IMPORTANT lists. All of the time. IMPORTANTLY.

Rule 5: Get a little bit muddy down the brook (but NOT in pointy shoes).

Rule 6: Practice making home-made sticky flapjack—so that you can have a lot in common with your friends.

And please remember: EVERYONE should be allowed in the *Giggle-Wheeze Gang* because NOBODY likes to feel left out.

Make sure your invisible dog joins the gang too

This is me—not being left out at all!!!!

HOW TO MAKE SUPER STICKY FLAPJACK

250g Porridge Oats

125g Butter

125g Brown Sugar

2-3 tbsps Golden Syrup

(**2 tablespoons** for normal stickiness,

but **3 tablespoons** if you want it to get

stuck in your teeth. And please sprinkle

in squidgy sultanas if you like that sort

of thing).

EXTRA BITS THAT ARE A TOTAL SURPRISE

♥ Melt the butter, syrup, and sugar in a pan.

♥ Stir in the oats (and sultanas if you like them).

♥ Put all the mixture on a lightly-greased tray
or on baking paper and squish down with
a wooden spoon.

♥ Cook at 180°C/Gas Mark 4 for about
20 minutes.

♥ Let it cool and go a bit crunchy.

♥ Put on a spotty plate or something similar.

♥ Share with a friend who lives in completely
the RIGHT house.

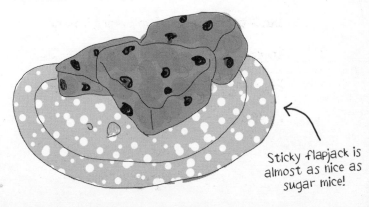

Sticky flapjack is
almost as nice as
sugar mice!

BiT TWO:

♥

WENDY QUiLL'S
HOW TO STOP WORRYING
WHEN YOU CAN'T

♥ The first thing to do is not even think about it.

♥ Then, sit on all of your hands.

♥ Now you are sitting on your hands, you can stop worrying about biting your nails because it will actually be quite tricky!

This is what NOT-thinking looks like

♥ If your nails sneak into your mouth when you're not looking, just remember to completely ignore them.

♥ If you have a little nibble by mistake, don't worry about it at all (because worrying is the thing you're not supposed to do).

Here are some nails I bit earlier. (When I wasn't looking!)

FAMOUS PEOPLE WHO BIT THEIR NAILS*
(A VERY IMPORTANT LIST)

Napoleon

Elvis Presley

Marilyn Monroe

Britney Spears

Robbie Williams

Prince Harry

Shakespeare
(but this is only a guess because he might have just been chewing his sleeve)

Harry Potter

💜 But if you keep biting them by accident, why not chew your sleeve a bit instead?

* I am actually finding this list a bit tricky —so if you can think of any more famous nail biters, please email them to me at **wendywheezybirdquill@gmail.com**

ABOUT THE AUTHOR AND THE ILLUSTRATOR

WENDY MEDDOUR very slightly squashed someone the first time she went out on her brand-new, second-hand bike. She also got into trouble for going to completely the wrong house and giving flapjack to completely the wrong Jemima! But she NEVER read anybody's diary. Not even once. Well. Only a tiny bit. And that was only because a ghost made her do it!

When no one was looking . . . Mina May added Mrs Bennett, Benjamina, a bell on the bike, and a helmet

HISTORICAL EVIDENCE: this is an actual photograph of Wendy Meddour on the bike that did the squashing!

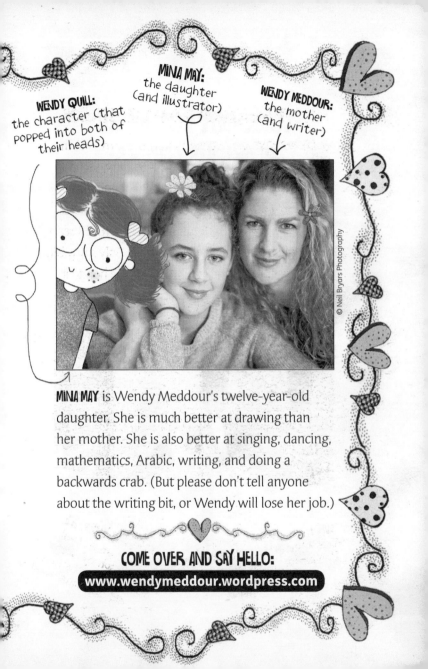

WENDY QUILL:
the character (that popped into both of their heads)

MINA MAY:
the daughter (and illustrator)

WENDY MEDDOUR:
the mother (and writer)

© Neil Bryars Photography

MINA MAY is Wendy Meddour's twelve-year-old daughter. She is much better at drawing than her mother. She is also better at singing, dancing, mathematics, Arabic, writing, and doing a backwards crab. (But please don't tell anyone about the writing bit, or Wendy will lose her job.)

COME OVER AND SAY HELLO:

www.wendymeddour.wordpress.com

LOOK OUT FOR MORE HILARIOUS CAPERS:

written by **WENDY MEDDOUR**
with drawings by **MINA MAY** AGE 11

WENDY QUILL
IS A CROCODILE'S BOTTOM

'It is a completely true fact that you will LOVE this book!'

written by **WENDY MEDDOUR**
with drawings by **MINA MAY** AGE 12

WENDY QUILL
TRIES TO GROW A PET

'You won't catch nits from reading this book but you'll definitely get the giggles!'